Jenny Heartfield's DILEMMA

A TALE OF DREAMS AND BETRAYAL

ATTICUS BLACKWOOD

Contents

Chapter 1

L oveland, Ohio, is a picturesque town nestled amidst breathtaking natural beauty, including majestic mountains and a diverse array of wildlife. Its storied history, tracing back to the 1800s, is reflected in its charming cobblestone streets, enchanting shops, and well-preserved historic architecture.

I'm Jenny Heartfield, and Loveland has been my home for as long as I can remember. Despite its small size, Loveland, Ohio, offers a wealth of experiences. The town is surrounded by sweeping hills, verdant forests, and a meandering river, creating an awe-inspiring landscape that never fails to captivate.

Nestled in the heart of Loveland, Ohio, lies a community unlike any other. This charming town is renowned for its strong sense of camaraderie and neighborly warmth. With its picturesque landscapes and vibrant cultural scene, Loveland is a place where tradition and modernity coalesce seamlessly, creating a truly unique experience. From leisurely walks through lush parks to partake in the town's rich tapestry of festivals, there's an abundance of activities to enjoy. Whether it's casting a line in the tranquil river or savoring diverse culinary delights, Loveland never fails to captivate and inspire. At its core, Loveland isn't just a place to reside; it's a tapestry of cherished memories and enduring friendships, forever etched in the fabric of our lives.

Every morning presented a daunting challenge as I reluctantly pried myself from the warmth of my cocoon-like bed and made my way to the window. There, I was greeted by an awe-inspiring sight: the sun's radiant beams dancing off the grand mountain range, casting a golden sheen across the mist-covered hills. This breath-taking view had been a steadfast presence in my life for a remarkable 18 years, yet each day, it continued to evoke feelings of pure amazement and curiosity within me. The sweet fragrance of daylilies wafted in from the backyard, infusing my room with an air of anticipation and joy. Regrettably, the time to head to school approached, marking the conclusion of my tranquil morning reflections.

As the sunlight streams through my window, signaling the start of a new day, I rouse myself from slumber and make a beeline for the shower. The sensation of warm water cascading over me is both invigorating and soothing, preparing me for the day ahead. Stepping out, I confront my unruly blonde locks in the mirror, attempting to rein them in with a comb and my nimble fingers.

I then take stock of my pallid complexion, begging for a touch of vitality. A dollop of moisturizer is my first line of defense, revitalizing my skin and imparting a much-needed glow. A quick teeth-brushing session is followed by a subtle application of makeup, just enough to accentuate my natural features and bolster my confidence for the day.

As I make my way to my computer, my heart races with anticipation. I'm eager to check my email inbox, hoping that today will be the day I receive a message from Columbia University regarding my college application. The past two weeks have been filled with nervous anticipation as I wait for news that could change my life forever. The thought of not being accepted into the university and being unable to realize my dream of pursuing higher education has been weighing heavily on my mind. One email could bring me closer to realizing my dream of becoming a teacher and returning to my hometown, Loveland, to impart knowledge to the next generation of students.

I have the potential to be an invaluable source of support for students, just as my own teachers were for me. I was fortunate to have some truly outstanding teachers who went the extra mile to help me reach my goals. One teacher, in particular, made a profound impact on me. She consistently provided guidance and support whenever I sought her assistance, ultimately inspiring me to pursue a career in education.

I understand that the path to becoming a teacher is filled with obstacles. Despite the challenges that lie ahead, I am resolute in my determination to surmount them. My aspiration of becoming a teacher and returning to Loveland hinges on receiving a crucial letter for my admission to the school of my choice, without which my dream may remain unrealized. I eagerly anticipate its arrival in the hope that it will come soon.

As I completed my preparations, I hurried down the stairs to assist my mother, Heather Heartfield, with getting ready for work. Heather's lustrous, sun-kissed blonde hair flowed in gentle waves down her back, echoing my own. Her fair and delicate complexion complemented her tousled blonde hair, which bore the signs of some weight gain over the years. Nonetheless, her affable smile and unwavering confidence were truly admirable. She had endured significant emotional upheaval when my father departed, having met a younger woman while traveling cross-country as a truck driver.

Despite the challenging battle with weight gain and emotional distress, my mother would diligently make her way to her job at the potato processing factory every single day. It was not the job she had always dreamed of, but as a mother at 17 without a high school diploma, it was the only employment she could secure. During her moments of respite, my mother would often savor a glass of wine while following the latest episodes of The Bachelor, using it as a brief escape from the harsh realities of her life.

As I stood in the kitchen preparing our lunches, I observed my mother descending the stairs, dressed in her factory uniform, in search of her hairnet. Sensing her fatigue, I greeted her with concern, "Hey,

Mom, how are you feeling? Did you get any sleep last night?" she responded wearily, "No, not really. I had to work a double shift and got back very late. But I need the money, especially with your no-good father running around with some woman he met in Detroit." I tried to reassure her, "Well, we don't have to think about him anymore. He left, and we will do better without him." Despite my efforts to remain resolute, I deeply missed him. My mother managed a faint smile before resuming her search for the hairnet.

After I completed my usual morning routine, I escorted my mother to her car as she readied herself to head off to work. Her brows were furrowed with worry as she turned to me and said, "Jenny, I'll be even later coming home today. It's just not fair that I have to work so much, but we really need the extra income without your dad's contribution." I wasn't surprised by her words; she had been expressing the same concerns every day for the past few weeks. It was clear that she was still grappling with the aftermath of my father leaving despite the passing of time. As I watched her drive away, I collected my belongings and readied myself for my day ahead.

Our family-owned just one car, and it was typically used by my mom for work. This meant that I often relied on my boyfriend, Liam, for transportation. Liam had graduated from high school the previous year and was now working at his dad's paint shop. He spent his days driving around town, delivering gallons of paint to various clients. Liam was a tall, lanky young man with a strikingly handsome appearance. His vibrant red hair contrasted beautifully with his soft, inviting features and a charming smile that could light up any room. Despite being the three-time prom king and the most popular boy at our school, he chose to be with me, which always amazed me. Our love story began when I was a freshman, and he was a sophomore. I remember the day he asked me out for ice cream, and as we strolled and chatted, he finally asked me to be his girlfriend. From that moment, we became inseparable, and every second we spent with him felt like a dream. He was my universe, and the thought of a future together kept my hopes high. I often pictured us getting married in the picturesque town of Loveland, surrounded by nature's beauty, and raising our children with all the love in the world. Thinking about our future always brought a sense of joy and optimism to my heart.

Liam welcomed me with a gentle grin, affectionately addressing me as "Sweetheart." He inquired if I was prepared for school or if I wished to accompany him on his delivery rounds. I eagerly hopped into his father's overloaded work van, which was packed with numerous paint cans stacked in the back. Liam drove cautiously due to the excessive load, affording us ample time to catch up. During our ride, he expressed concern about my mother, who was dealing with my father's departure. The mention of my father's abandonment stirred a pang in my chest, but I didn't want to burden anyone else with my troubles. I put on a forced smile and replied, "She's still upset but managing. She'll get over it eventually; we must give her time."

Although Liam looked at me with concern, he didn't delve further into the matter. Instead, we discussed my post-graduation plans, with me choosing to keep my application to Columbia University a secret. I didn't want to raise anyone's hopes if I didn't get in. As we neared my school, Liam pulled over at the curb. Despite the parking lot being just a few yards away, he insisted on dropping me off at the front of the school, radiating with pride as he escorted his "little sweetheart." His charming smile caused my cheeks to flush as he inquired about picking me up after my shift. "Yes, please. I'll be done at 6. Will that work for you?" I responded, attempting to conceal my excitement. "Of course, Sweetheart. I'll always make time for you," he assured, his smile widening. After rolling up his windows, he drove away, leaving me with the Combs blasting from his car.

As I gazed at the receding figure of Liam's car on the sidewalk, my heart pounded with anticipation. At that moment, my phone vibrated with an incoming email, sparking a surge of nerves and hope within me. I quickly checked my inbox and saw an email from the University of Colombia. As I immersed myself in the lengthy message, my eyes eagerly scanned each word until I reached the conclusion. "Congratulations, Ms. Heartfield," it read, "you have been accepted on a full scholarship to the University of Colombia. We look forward to seeing you this fall." Overwhelmed with joy, I let out an exuberant scream, drawing the attention of passers-by. Their curious stares didn't faze me in the least; I had finally achieved my dreams. The journey toward pursuing my passion for teaching would commence soon as I embarked on my college education.

Chapter 2

Upon receiving the astounding news, my heart brimmed with over-whelming excitement. At that moment, I knew exactly who I wanted to share this incredible news with first. With a fervent pace, I hurried down the hallway to seek out the one person who had been my un-wavering source of support - the individual who had ignited within me the aspiration to pursue a career in teaching: none other than our beloved English teacher, Mrs. Wash.

Mrs. Wash possessed an arresting presence, her long, fiery red hair flowing gracefully down her shoulders. Her slender form exuded a radiant glow, complemented by her tanned brown skin. However, it was her remarkable red hair that truly distinguished her, always styled in exquisite waves that seemed to glisten under the light. Throughout the years, I had been a part of her class, witnessing firsthand the transformative impact she had on her students' lives and her ability to instill unwavering hope for a brighter future. She instilled in us the belief that with dedication, anything was achievable. Moreover, it was Mrs. Wash who played a pivotal role in my decision to apply to Columbia University. Her guidance was instrumental in helping me complete the "New

Youth Scholarship application," which ultimately paved the way for my educational journey. This prestigious scholarship was bestowed upon students who were hailed as the new hope of our generation.

I hurried into her room, almost stumbling over my own feet. She looked up, a worried expression on her face as if she sensed something had gone awry. "Child, what's wrong? Are you okay?" she asked with concern. "Nothing's wrong, Mrs. Wash. It's just the opposite. I have received the most incredible news of my life," I exclaimed with excitement. I shared the details of the email I had received, and we both erupted in joyful screams, jumping around in her room. "This is wonderful, my dear. You are embarking on a new journey and getting closer to your dreams," she said with a radiant smile.

"Thank you, Mrs. Wash. You gave me the courage to pursue this. If it wasn't for you, I wouldn't have obtained the scholarship," I expressed, embracing her tightly. "Child, this is your achievement. I simply guided you to the opportunity, and you seized it," she replied, always offering encouraging words. "Thank you, Mrs. Wash. I need to find Harper and share the news with her, too," I announced, ready to dash off. However, she stopped me and pointed out, "Um, child, can't you see the time? You're going to be late for class." She was right. I didn't have the luxury of seeking out Harper or risking being tardy. I'd catch up with her during study hall at our usual spot. "Thank you once again, Mrs. Wash.

I will always appreciate everything you've done for me," I said, heading out. From the corner of my eye, I caught a glimpse of her smiling through tears streaming down her cheeks.

After enduring four long and tiresome classes, I finally made it to study hall, the highlight of my school day. Every afternoon, like clockwork, I would rendezvous with my closest friend, Harper, in the serene school courtyard, seeking refuge beneath the comforting shade of an imposing tree. Sharing my latest revelations with her always filled me with an uncontainable sense of excitement and happiness. Harper and I had been the closest of friends since our early days in first grade, and our bond was unbreakable. Despite her naturally introverted demeanor, she had always been a steadfast and encouraging companion. We had made a solemn vow to always be by each other's side. We dreamt of remaining in Loveland for eternity, growing old together, and watching our children grow up as neighbors. Our plans included attending the local community college and earning our associate degrees. I had no doubt that she would be thrilled to hear my news.

The sun bathed the world in its warm glow as I ventured outside, feeling its gentle caress on my face and the whisper of a cool breeze in my hair. My eyes found my best friend, Harper, nestled under the massive oak tree, munching on an apple and engrossed in a book. Eager to share my news, I hurried over to her. As I leaned in, Harper instinctively drew back, making it clear that she valued her personal space. Brushing off the subtle rebuff, I began sharing my excitement, but Harper's reaction stunned me. Instead of sharing in my joy, she seemed upset and angry. Perplexed, I inquired about her feelings. Harper's voice trembled as she expressed her distress, saying, "Why would I be happy about my best friend leaving me behind?" Bewildered, I pressed for an explanation. "You and I promised we'd be together forever," she exclaimed with rising emotion. "But now you're leaving me for something better. You'll make new connections, forget about me, and never return."

Her words hit me like a wave of cold water. I couldn't fathom that my best friend would react this way. "That's not true," I insisted. "I'm going to college to become a teacher and return to help our community. Our friendship will endure no matter where we are." But Harper remained unconvinced. She was plagued by the fear of being left behind and forgotten, and I couldn't shake the guilt of causing her pain.

Harper's voice quivered with pain and disappointment as she confronted me, "Why did you choose to keep this from me? I thought we were best friends, inseparable since childhood. And now, at the first opportunity, you're abandoning me. What kind of friend does that?"

I was taken aback by her words, unsure of how to respond. "Harper, you know how much our friendship means to me. Why are you saying this?" I struggled to maintain my composure, feeling my emotions intensify with each passing moment.

"How can I be friends with someone who would deceive me and then act as if leaving is some favor to me?" Harper's bitterness resurfaced in her tone. "You're heading off to college, forgetting about us, and never looking back. And just because you claim we'll stay friends, for how long? Until you stop responding to my messages or avoiding my calls? Do you think your new college friends will be better than me? Do you think anyone will care for you as deeply as I do? Do you believe anyone else will want to support you and your family issues?"

The words that Harper spoke cut deep, like shards of glass slicing through my heart, plunging me into a dark abyss of emotional turmoil. I had carried the heavy burden of my father's abandonment alone, not even sharing it with my closest friend, Liam. And now, Harper, who had once been my closest confidante, was casting doubt on my moral compass and taking aim at my dreams of going to college. Her jealousy was palpable, etched into every line of her face. As I confronted her, I expressed how much I valued our friendship and implored her not to let my upcoming departure destroy what we had built. I reminded her of all the cherished memories we had shared under our favorite tree and expressed my hopes of preserving our bond despite the physical distance. Ultimately, I made it clear that I hadn't chosen to end our friendship - that decision was hers to make.

Harper and I were sitting on a bench in the school courtyard, surrounded by the sound of chirping birds and rustling leaves. I noticed a sudden shift in Harper's demeanor as tears began to well up in her eyes. Instinctively, I reached out to comfort her by placing my hand on her shoulder, but she violently pushed it away. Then, without warning, she uttered deeply hurtful words that cut through me like a knife. Her accusation that I was a selfish friend who only cared about myself, followed by a cruel mention of my father, left me speechless, my eyes widening in shock. Before I could gather my thoughts, she hastily gathered her belongings and stormed off, leaving me in a state of disbelief. As she disappeared into the school building, her parting glare conveyed a depth of anger and hurt that I had never seen from her before. Watching her leave, I couldn't hold back my tears. It dawned on me that I may have lost my best friend at that moment, and the thought of ever regaining her trust felt like an insurmountable challenge.

Chapter 3

As I stepped out of the school gates, the weight of the recent events pressed down on me like a physical force. Each step I took on my regular 10-minute walk to work felt like an arduous journey through thick, unyielding mud. It was as though the entirety of my shattered friendship had been placed squarely upon my shoulders, the burden almost unbearable. Every breath I drew felt strained, and each movement seemed to demand an enormous effort. I was engulfed by the overwhelming heaviness of what had un-folded at school.

As I made my way through downtown, I couldn't help but notice the concerned expressions on the faces of the familiar locals. It was as if they could sense that something was amiss. Even Ms. Jackson, the kind-hearted florist, attempted to halt me, her worry apparent. I mustered a fee-ble smile and assured her that everything was fine. The remainder of my journey to work was no less challenging. Living in a close-knit community meant that every-one was akin to extended family, attuned to any deviations from the norm. Despite my efforts to appear composed, I couldn't help feeling as though every gaze was fixed upon me, silently assessing me. Nevertheless, I pressed on, determined to reach my workplace.

After spending four years as a waitress at the Loveland Diner, a cozy downtown establishment, the time has come for me to bid farewell. My tenure at the diner has been incredibly fulfilling, allowing me to contribute to my community in a small yet meaningful manner. During my time there, I had the pleasure of witnessing warm family gatherings, friends catching up over burgers, and the endearing sight of Mrs. Walsh visiting to check in on me and grab a hearty meal for her husband, a local police officer with a robust appetite. Working at the Loveland Diner has been much more than a job; it has been an opportunity to forge connections and positively impact the lives of those around me.

With plans to enroll in school at the end of summer, I must soon inform my boss, Mr. Ross, about my impending departure. I am hopeful that the conversation will be far smoother than the recent one I had with Harper.

Mr. Ross was a commanding figure in his late 40s, known for his towering height and larger-than-life personality. Standing at least 7 feet tall, his presence was unmistakable, and his balding head was a distinctive feature he carried with pride. Despite his physical stature, he was approachable and had a reputation for being confident and charismatic. He was the proud owner of Loveland Diner, a family business that had been passed down through five generations. He always showed kindness to me, especially during tough times when he allowed me to work extra hours after my dad left. However, breaking the news to him about leaving for college would be a daunting task.

Before I could gather the courage to visit his office, Emma, a familiar face at Loveland Diner, intercepted me to inquire about my well-being. Emma, a 26-year-old mother of three, worked as a waitress at the diner for the past seven years. Despite her petite and plump appearance, she exuded a vitality that I envied. Her journey into motherhood began during high school when she became pregnant by her boyfriend, who coincidentally worked at the same potato processing factory as my mom did. Despite the challenges she faced, Emma remained a dedicated and cheerful waitress, always ready with a warm smile to welcome customers and take their orders.

As I began my collaboration with Emma, she took me under her wing and familiarized me with the ins and outs of the job. I was appreciative of her guidance, but I quickly realized that I couldn't align with her methods of trying to garner larger tips from the customers. Despite this disparity in our views, I maintained a respectful attitude towards her as a colleague and valued the initial assistance she provided.

"Are you okay? You look upset," she inquired, adjusting her vibrant, attention-grabbing glasses. "If you want to earn good tips, you need to tidy up," I assured her that I was fine and then proceeded to confide in her about my recent disagreement with Harper. Her eyes widened like a

deer caught in headlights before she finally spoke up, "That's unbelievable. Would
she really end your friendship just because
you're going to college?" I responded with
a shrug. "I'll give it a few days before trying
to reach out to her. I'm sure things will
settle down, and we can resolve this," I said.
She glanced around as more customers began to arrive. "Let's continue this conversation later," she said as she picked up some
menus and a notepad to take orders. While
she was occupied, I went to Mr. Ross's office.

As I stepped into his secluded office,
I found him engrossed in his computer
screen. Given the location of his restaurant
and the popularity of the burger and fries
combo, I assumed he was placing orders
for potatoes or ground beef. His eyes lit

up as he noticed me, and he greeted me with an exuberant smile, "How is my favorite employee doing this evening? Oh, Jenny, you look stressed. Did something happen?" I reassured him that everything was fine and then shared the life-changing news of my acceptance into Columbia University.

His initial joy for me was evident as he exclaimed, "That's amazing, Jenny! I'm so proud of you," and promptly rose from behind his desk to engulf me in a heart-felt hug. However, his expression turned somber as the realization dawned on him that my transition to college would mean leaving my job. "Well, I guess this day was going to come. Please promise me that you will continue to work through the summer before you leave," he said with a tinge of sadness.

I mustered a smile and assured him, "Of course, I'll be here." He then asked if there was anything he could do to make me stay, expressing how indispensable I was as an employee and contemplating how the place would run without me. My response was heartfelt, "You guys will be just fine without me. But I will miss working here and working for you."

He gazed up at the ceiling with a contemplative expression before saying, "Well, if there is anything I can do to change your mind, let me know. Now, you should change your shift as it is about to start." I embraced him one more time and made my way to the locker room to don my waitress uniform, a classic 80s style ensemble featuring light blue tops and plain white aprons with our names embroidered in bright red cursive letters on the right breast pocket.

The shift unfolded in its usual rhythm, with some regular customers ordering their familiar dishes. As the day wound down and the closing time approached, Emma approached me, inquiring about the earlier event. "Wow, that is crazy. I'm sorry that happened to you, but maybe it's for the best," she remarked, her attention split between our conversation and the tips she had earned that night. Mr. Ross walked over to us with his characteristic wide grin. "Jenny, I've figured it out. I know what I could offer you to stay here. How about becoming the new Manager of Loveland Diner?" His eyes sparkled with anticipation, but Emma beside me did not mirror the same sentiment.

Emma's eyes blazed with fury as she confronted Mr. Ross. "Wait a minute, Mr. Ross. Are you seriously going to offer the Manager position to her before offering it to me?" Mr. Ross's usually jovial expression vanished as he turned to face her. "Well, Emma, I acknowledge that you've been with us the longest, but I haven't seen the drive and ambition required for the manager role. I also have reservations about your methods of soliciting extra tips from our male patrons. On the other hand, Jenny embodies the qualities of an exemplary manager. She's consistently punctual, and her dedication is evident in the extra hours she puts in to ensure that everything is in order before she leaves. Jenny, would you be interested in the position?" Before Jenny could respond, Emma leaped to her feet. "This is ridiculous! This girl is barely old enough to file her taxes, let alone manage an entire restaurant. She can't even leave her personal drama at home; she wears it on her face and elicits sympathy from everyone. I don't believe she's emotionally stable for this job, especially after her father left her for someone else. And now, you want her to oversee your business instead of me? I'm the ideal candidate. I manage three kids and a husband. I could run this place in my sleep. And if you have an issue with how I secure extra tips, then perhaps you should consider paying me more." Mr. Ross and Jenny exchanged uneasy glances. It was the second time that day someone had brought up Jenny's father, a subject she had kept hidden and internalized. Emma's implication that Jenny couldn't handle the managerial role incensed her. She knew she consistently contributed more to the restaurant's operations than Emma, even covering Emma's shifts when she was too hungover to come to work. Before Jenny could defend herself, Mr. Ross intervened. "Now, Ms. Emma, if you feel that way, perhaps I can resolve your concerns by letting you go." Emma stepped closer, her voice rising. "Are you threatening to fire me? Are you out of your mind?" Mr. Ross's tone turned stern. "No, Ms. Emma. I'm perfectly lucid, and I suggest you reconsider your position here."

I stood up, feeling a surge of adrenaline, and positioned myself firmly between Mr.

Ross and Emma. They were both in the midst of a heated argument, and I knew it was time for me to speak up. Keeping my voice steady and composed, I turned to address Mr. Ross directly. "Mr. Ross, I want to express my gratitude for the opportunity, but I've made a firm decision to pursue college. I believe it's only fair to offer the position to Emma, given her financial responsibilities as a mother."

As I shifted my gaze towards Emma, I struggled to contain the hurt and betrayal that welled up within me. It was difficult to look her in the eyes as I continued, "However, let it be clear, Emma, I advocate for you solely based on your family circumstances, not your qualifications for the role."

Emma had always been like a supportive older sister to me, but the revelation of her actions stung deeply. Despite the tumult of emotions I was feeling, I made a conscious effort to maintain my composure. Addressing Mr. Ross once more, I continued with resolve, "I regret to inform you, Mr. Ross, that today marks my departure. I cannot continue working in an environment tainted by such disloyalty. I apologize for any inconvenience, but tomorrow will not see my return."

Turning towards Emma, I struggled with the urge to convey my feelings of disappointment and resentment, but instead managed to utter, "And Emma, please relay my message to your children, letting them know I played a part in securing a better opportunity for their mother."

I removed my apron, feeling the weight of the day's events heavy on my shoulders. With a heavy heart, I handed it to Mr. Ross, silently signaling the end of an era. As I slung my backpack over my shoulder and headed for the door, a tumult of emotions swirled within me. Just before I stepped outside, I caught a glimpse of Emma's indifferent reflection in the glass door. In that fleeting moment, it became clear to me that our shared history meant nothing to her. Despite the bittersweet mix of emotions that flooded my being, I knew that this departure would mark the end of an era for me.

Chapter 4

Reluctantly, with a heavy heart and a sense of unease, I turned my back on Loveland Diner, feeling a pang of regret as I walked away. I couldn't shake the feeling that I had made the wrong decision. The prospect of dealing with Emma's hostility had become unbearable, and I knew I couldn't continue working with her. The thought of spending the rest of the summer around her filled me with dread. As I made my way down the street, memories of my time at the diner flooded my mind.

The lingering smells of bacon and coffee, the familiar sound of clinking plates, and the jovial laughter of patrons all seemed to taunt me. I hoped my boss, Mr. Ross, would understand my reasons for leaving, but I knew it was too late to go back and explain myself. I had quit, and my pride wouldn't allow me to reconsider. Despite the sadness and regret that weighed heavily on me, I knew I had made the right decision. I couldn't let the toxic atmosphere at work continue to impact my mental well-being, especially with college just weeks away.

I anticipated my mom's disapproval of my choice, but I hoped she would be more understanding when I revealed that I had earned a scholarship to college. Rounding the corner, a sense of relief washed over me. I was eager to reunite with Liam, my boyfriend, and share everything that had transpired. He was my unwavering support, and I was confident he would be elated for me, regardless of the circumstances.

After finishing work, I always eagerly anticipated my rendezvous with Liam at our special spot where we shared our first kiss: a charming old-fashioned lamppost at the corner of downtown in the historic district. It was a delightful little area, just a short distance from Loveland Diner. As I strolled toward the lamppost, a wave of comfort and nostalgia washed over me. The short walk allowed me some precious moments to clear my head.

My mind was preoccupied with a myriad of thoughts. I had recently received some wonderful news before the start of school, but it seemed like the only person gen-uinely thrilled for me was Ms. Wash, my English teacher. To compound my unease, I had a fallout with my best friend over a frivolous notion that we might not remain friends if I left. This trivial argument left me feeling distraught and bewildered. As if this weren't enough, I found myself torn between pursuing a managerial position for higher pay and following my dream of becoming a teacher by going to college. The weight of this pivotal decision loomed over me, unsettling my mind.

The day had already been overwhelm-ing, and it didn't help when my colleague, Emma, made a hurtful comment about my stability at work because of my dad's ab-sence. It was an old wound that she ca-sually prodded, and it stung more than I cared to admit. Harper had also brought up my dad today, despite his abandonment of my mom and me a while ago. It was a sore subject, and I had been trying my best to be resilient for my mom. I didn't want to burden anyone with my emotions, but it seemed like everyone could see right through my facade and tell how much I was hurting.

Amid all the turmoil, seeing Liam waiting at the light post made my heart flutter. Sitting on a bench, enjoying his ice cream, he looked as enchanting as ever. It was a brief moment of bliss on an otherwise distressing day.

Approaching Liam, my heart raced with both nerves and relief. Sitting down beside him, he leaned in and gently kissed my forehead, and at that moment, my worries and fears seemed to dissolve. He asked about my day, and as I took a deep breath, I poured my heart out to him. I shared every detail — from the euphoria of being accepted into college to the distress of Harper's betrayal and the tension with Emma at work. It was a lot to unload, but I knew Liam would stand by me no matter what. As I finished speaking, I looked at him, expecting words of comfort or reassurance. To my astonishment, he just gazed at the ground with a vacant expression.

Under the glow of the bright streetlight, Liam interjected the quiet with a question about my plans for college. As he gazed down at the pavement, he inquired, "So, you're really going to college?" Filled with anticipation, I nodded and replied, "Yes, I'm heading off at the end of the summer." Eager to spend more time together before my departure, I suggested a road trip to New York City for some memorable adventures. With a hopeful grin, I proposed finding a special spot where we could hang out whenever he visited, perhaps a charming restaurant or another picturesque streetlight like the one illuminating our conversation.

However, Liam's response caught me off guard. Still fixated on the ground, he questioned, "Why would I even do that? Why should I drive all the way to New York?" Confused, I reminded him, "Because you're my boyfriend." His reply was frosty, "Oh, now I'm your boyfriend. I wasn't your boyfriend when you applied for college." His expression was a mix of annoyance and hurt.

I attempted to convey that Mrs. Wash and I had made a mutual decision not to disclose our relationship to avoid raising anyone's expectations. However, Liam's response was heated. "Oh, it's Mrs. Wash's doing, isn't it? That old lady never approved of me; she always thought you were too good for me. But she's just envious. No one like me ever paid her any attention."

I rose to my feet and asserted myself, a mix of anger and confusion swirling within me. "Don't speak about Mrs. Wash in that manner," I stated firmly. "She has always been supportive of me and has had my best interests at heart." Liam's face twisted in rage, and his eyes gleamed dangerously. "What's gotten into you?" I inquired, attempting to maintain composure. "Why are you becoming so incensed?"

As he spoke, I saw the anger in his eyes intensify. "I'm getting angry," he said through gritted teeth, "because my girlfriend decided to leave for higher learning because of some teacher that can't stay out of your life." His accusation took me aback. "What are you talking about?" I asked, trying to make sense of his words. But Liam didn't seem interested in explanations. His anger grew increasingly intense, and I started to feel scared. I stepped back, but he lunged forward and grabbed my arm. "Jenny, are you not happy with me?" he demanded, his voice rising. "Don't I make you happy?"

I didn't know what to say. Liam had never acted like this before, and I felt overwhelmed by his sudden outburst. All I could do was shake my head, hoping he would let me go.

My heart was pounding as I looked up at him, fear coursing through me. "Yes, you make me happy, but now you're scaring and hurting me," I exclaimed. His grip on my arm tightened, causing me to wince in pain. "Please let go of me," I pleaded, attempting to pull away. Instead of releasing me, he squeezed even tighter.

"Do you really believe you can do better than me, Jenny?" he sneered, his face contorted with anger. "Is that what Mrs. Wash has filled your head with? Do you think you'll find someone better than me in New York?" I shook my head, tears streaming down my face. "No, I don't think that," I whimpered. "I just want you to stop hurting me."

He refused to listen, his voice growing louder. "Do you really think someone else will put up with you better than I do?" he questioned. "You act so superior, but you're just a burden to me. I have to deal with your issues all the time." In response, I pushed him away, feeling a surge of anger. "What are you even talking about?" I exclaimed. "Am I a burden to you? I never trouble you with anything." Instead of responding, he simply laughed, releasing his hold on me and walking away, leaving me feeling alone and fearful. "Is that what you really think? Do you believe everyone treats you like a child out of pity for you since your dad left?" he continued. "You wander around like a lost puppy, on the verge of tears at any hint of criticism. And now you're talking about going to college.

I spent four years protecting you and looking out for you. Did you think I wanted to stay with the odd girl abandoned by her father for someone else? He's probably happier with his new partner while watching your mom waste away. But I stayed because I love you, and what did you do the first chance you got? You left me behind for something new. I guess you and your dad have something in common."

I was utterly stunned. My boyfriend of four years, Liam, had betrayed me, just as Harper and Emma had. I couldn't comprehend what was happening. Was I in a dream? This had to be a nightmare; it couldn't be real. "I can't believe what you're saying, Liam. This isn't like you," I begged, desperately hoping that Liam would snap out of it. Instead, he just let out a mocking laugh and gazed down at me with a smug expression on his face.

"See what did I say? Like a sad puppy ready to cry. You know what? Go ahead and run off to college. You won't make it there without me, and you'll be running back here in about a month. When you return, I won't be waiting for you, so you'll be alone. Meanwhile, I will have found someone who meets my needs without causing me to feel like I need to tip-toe around them." he said, his voice dripping with contempt.

I found myself staring at Liam in utter shock and disbelief as if the ground had crumbled beneath my feet. He had always been my unwavering support, my partner in all adventures, my entire world. But now, it was as if an imposter had taken over his body, someone unrecognizable to me. As he turned his back and began to walk towards his paint van, abandoning me in my anguish, I stood frozen in place, unable to comprehend or process what had just unfolded.

"Are you serious? You're just going to discard me so easily? Do those four years mean nothing to you?" I couldn't help but raise my voice, my words echoing through the empty street, with no one around to witness the shattering of my heart.

His gaze locked with mine as he swung open the car door and settled into the seat. The weight of the silence enveloped us, suffocating any trace of sound. Then, he broke the stillness, his voice a turbulent mix of frustration, disillusionment, and sorrow, "All I can think right now is that

I've invested four years trying to love someone incapable of reciprocating." His words hung in the air before he spoke again, his tone gentler this time, "It's over, darling. Enjoy New York." With that, he ignited the engine and vanished into the distance, leaving me alone in the heart of the city; collapsed on the sidewalk, tears streaming down my face. The world seemed to recede as I struggled to comprehend the sudden turn of events. The anguish of losing someone I held so dearly was nearly insufferable, and I felt my heart shattering into countless fragments.

Chapter 5

Today has been an emotional whirlwind, and it feels like everything has taken a turn for the worse. The day started with an incredible high when I received some life-changing news, but it quickly transformed into a nightmare. It all began with a disagreement with my close friend Harper, who accused me of selfishness for wanting to pursue college away from home. Her words cut deep because we've been friends since childhood, and I never expected her to turn against me.

At work, I was overjoyed to be offered a well-deserved promotion, but the joy was tarnished by a coworker's outburst. She was deeply unhappy about my promotion, causing a scene that left a cloud of tension hanging in the air. Overwhelmed by the events of the day, I made a rash decision and quit my job, not knowing how else to handle the situation.

Adding to the chaos, my world shattered when the person I love most, Liam, abruptly ended our relationship in the most hurtful manner possible. His unexpected decision hit me with the force of a wrecking ball, leaving me at a loss for how to navigate the pain and uncertainty ahead.

These events have left me reeling, questioning everything about my future. Should I proceed with my plans to attend college in New York? Can I possibly move forward with my life in such disarray? Is it worth trying to mend things with Harper, or should I consider returning to my former job and pursuing the manager position? And then there's Liam - is it possible that his parting words were not genuine and that he still holds feelings for me?

As I sat on the bench beneath the flickering light post, tears streaming down my cheeks, the approaching bright lights caught my attention. The sound of tires halting in front of me made me lift my gaze to see Mrs. Wash stepping out of her familiar blue Toyota Prius. Relief washed over me as I recognized her, knowing I could confide in her. With a worried expression, she hurried over to me, asking what had brought me to tears in the darkness.

As she gently brushed my hair away from my face, I poured out my heart to her, recounting everything that had transpired since I last saw her that morning. With genuine concern in her eyes, she listened attentively, offering me her kind and comforting presence. At that moment, I felt a deep sense of trust and knew that I could confide in her without reservation.

After I finished speaking, Ms. Wash's eyes softened with compassion as she took in my words. "Oh, Jenny, I'm so sorry that all of this happened to you. This is more than any 18-year-old girl should go through in one day," she said gently. Her empathy was a balm to my raw emotions, but I still felt utterly lost and bewildered. I couldn't bring myself to meet her gaze as I turned my eyes away and confessed,

"Ms. Wash, I don't think I'm going to college. This was too much, and I can't leave everything broken like this. I need my best friend back, and I need Liam back. We love each other, and there has to be a way I can get him back."

Ms. Wash gently placed her hand under my chin, tilting my head upward to meet her gaze. "My dear, that would be the gravest mistake of your life," she said with a sincere expression. I furrowed my brows, struggling to comprehend her words. "Ms. Wash, with all due respect, how is not pursuing college and attempting to reclaim my life the worst mistake I could make?" I inquired, searching her eyes for an answer. Ms. Wash lifted her gaze to the night sky, a soft smile gracing her lips. "Dear, you possess remarkable intelligence, kindness, and empathy, but you put others' needs before your own. In life, we must sometimes make choices that appear self-centered to outsiders, yet they offer opportunities for personal growth."

The message from Ms. Wash really resonated with me. She reminded me that while relationships may come and go, it's important to prioritize living the life we truly deserve. She acknowledged the closeness between me and Harper, assuring me that a deep friendship like ours would endure any hardship. Ms. Wash also helped me see through Liam's facade, pointing out that he may have been driven by his own insecurities when he was with me. She questioned whether his feelings were genuine or merely based on the idea of being with someone like me, prompting me to consider the difference as I matured.

Ms. Wash's words made me realize that I needed to assert control over my own life and steer it in the direction I truly desired.

"I'll never forget those words," I recounted to Mrs. Wash. Her embrace was reassuring, and her smile warm. "Thank you, Mrs. Wash. You always knew the right thing to say to set me back on track," I expressed my gratitude. Eager to know how she had found me, I inquired. She simply motioned towards her car, and it was then that I noticed her husband in the driver's seat, grinning at me. Mrs. Wash explained that they were touring the historic district when she spotted me standing beneath the lamppost, prompting them to pull over. I felt overwhelmed with gratitude for their fortuitous intervention. As they drove away, I promised Mrs. Wash that I would make her proud. Her response was humble but resolute: "Don't make that promise to me. Make it for yourself. Now get in the car. We are taking you home," she grinned and said.

Upon hearing those words, a wave of realization washed over me. It dawned on me that I had completely neglected to broach the subject of my departure with my mother. As emotions ran high all around, I couldn't shake the feeling that my mother would be impacted the most. Having already endured my father's departure and lack of financial support, my leaving would only deepen her sense of heartbreak and abandonment. The thought of my mother feeling betrayed and turning against me was unbearable. While I understood Harper and Liam's responses, my mother's opinion held the greatest weight. She had always stood by me through thick and thin. However, the scars from my father's actions had left her embittered, angry, and sorrowful. Despite this, she was valiantly piecing together her life. The prospect of letting her down and causing her further anguish brought me to tears once more. Mrs. Wash, seated beside me, noticed my distress and inquired about the cause. I confessed that I had not spoken to my mother all day and fretted over her eventual reaction to my news. The fear of her turning her back on me was paralyzing. Comfortingly, Mrs. Wash took a gentle look at me and said, "Dear, let's head to the car. I believe your mother might surprise you."

Chapter 6

As I settled into the back seat of the car, I found myself surrounded by the reassuring presence of Mr. and Mrs. Wash in the front seats, with Mr. Wash confidently at the helm. The day had been an emotional rollercoaster, and my mind was racing with everything that had transpired. Despite Mrs. Wash's hopeful assurance that my mom would surprise me, I found it hard to share her optimism. The impending reaction of my mom to my decision to move to college in New York loomed heavily in my thoughts. I knew that my mom was still grappling with my dad's departure, and the notion of me leaving felt like a betrayal. It was challenging to envision a scenario in which she wouldn't be deeply upset or perhaps even inclined to sever our ties. The more I dwelled on it, the more fraught and apprehensive I felt. Would she be furious? Would she be distressed? Would she try to dissuade me from leaving? The weight of guilt and unease had been gnawing at me all day.

As the car journey stretched seemingly endlessly, I spent most of it gazing out of the window, taking in the distant mountains. Though they had always been a familiar sight, they somehow appeared different at that moment. Bathed in the moonlight, the rugged cliffs exuded an otherworldly, soothing, and promising aura.

Amidst the breathtaking beauty of my surroundings, a heavy cloud of sadness engulfed me, refusing to dissipate. I drew strength from the towering mountains in the distance, their unwavering presence a reminder to stand firm. The weight of the impending challenges ahead felt almost suffocating.

In a moment of solace, Mrs. Wash cast a gentle glance back at me, her eyes brimming with empathy. Summoning a faint smile, I nodded in acknowledgment, finding solace in her reassuring presence. Mr. Wash steered the car with steady assurance, and the rhythmic hum of the engine provided a comforting backdrop to our hushed conversation.

Despite the lingering apprehension, the company of the Washes in the car offered a respite from the grip of loneliness. Their compassion and unwavering support infused me with the fortitude to confront whatever lay ahead.

As we pulled up to my house, I noticed my mom's car already parked in the driveway. It struck me that I had been out much later than planned; my legs felt like lead, making it difficult to move. I quietly hoped that my mom wouldn't be angry with me. She was the only person who still showed me care, and I didn't want to damage our relationship over a mere dream. Mrs. Wash, who had given me a ride, stepped out of her car and opened my door, motioning for me to follow her. I was surprised, thinking she was just dropping me off. Confused, I got out of the car and asked her, "Wait, Mrs. Wash, I thought you were dropping me off?" She turned to me and replied, "I told you your mother might surprise you."

We approached the door, and Mrs. Wash rapped on it and pressed the doorbell. My mom, clad in her pink panther pajamas, opened the door and was taken aback to see us at such a late hour. "Sarah, what are you doing here? Wait, Jenny, where have you been? Do you realize what time it is? I've been worried sick!" My mom expressed concern about my whereabouts. I was taken aback to hear Mrs. Wash address my mom as Sarah; I had never known her first name. "Heather, we have some news that you'll want to hear." Mrs. Wash's proud tone caught my attention, and my mom's expression began to change. "Wait, Sarah, did she get in? Is my baby going to college?" Mrs. Wash hugged my mom and exclaimed, "Jenny got accepted on a full scholarship; yes, your baby is going to college." Overwhelmed, my mother sank to the floor, weeping into Mrs. Wash's embrace, while I stood there feeling bewildered.

Mrs. Wash and I had made a secret pact not to disclose my college application to anyone. To my astonishment, my mother somehow discovered the truth. "Can someone explain what's happening here? Mom, how did you find out about my college application? I didn't tell anyone about it," I questioned. My mom rose from her seat, wearing a smile on her face. Mrs. Wash stepped in and clarified that she had to inform my mother since she was my legal guardian and would need to provide her signature for my scholarship. They both agreed that it was best for me not to be aware of their decision in order to boost my confidence in applying independently. Mrs. Wash had purposely kept this information from me to prevent my friends from influencing my decision. My mother turned to Mrs. Wash and inquired, "What was it that you mentioned earlier today?"

We entered the house and sank into the plush, comfortable couch. Mr. Wash stayed in the car, seemingly content, while his wife attempted to offer assistance. I poured out my heart to my mom about everything that had unfolded that day: Harper leaving, the tumult at work, and the breakup with Liam. "Good riddance to that Liam boy. I never really cared for him. He reminded me too much of your father. It's no surprise that he would react poorly to you trying to better yourself. Maybe if he applied himself, he wouldn't be stuck delivering paint cans for his father. As for Harper, she'll come around. Just give her some space. Hearing that your best friend is leaving, especially when you both pledged to stay in Loveland forever, must have been hard for her." My mom's perspective on Harper seemed plausible; perhaps I just needed to give her the space she required. However, that didn't excuse her hurtful behavior. "Harper might be upset, but that's no reason to bring up my dad and call me selfish." My mom placed her hand on my shoulder. "Jenny, you and Harper are young, and you might not fully understand the impact of your words on the people you care about. She's hurting right now, processing the fact that her best friend in the world is leaving, and she's afraid that you might make new friends and not come back." I grasped my mom's perspective. "But Harper knows me; she should understand that I wouldn't abandon her for new friends. That's just ridiculous," I murmured, gazing down at the floor. "Well, you didn't expect Liam to break up with you, but he did," Mrs. Wash interjected, and I glanced up at her. "People change, dear, or they reveal their true selves in the end, so it's not surprising that Harper felt the way she did. But don't concern yourself too much with Harper. She's also one of my bright students, and I have a surprise for her in the morning." I was puzzled by Mrs. Wash's mention of a surprise for Harper, but I decided to leave it be.

I gazed back at my mom, worry etched on my face. "But what about you? Will you be alright with me leaving? You'll be alone here." My mom's smile was radiant as she reassured me, "Jenny, I will be more than okay. I'm overjoyed that you've earned a scholarship to college. It's the best news I've received in a long time, maybe even in my whole life. I know I haven't done a great job of hiding my feelings after your dad left, but those are my feelings towards him. I would never let them affect you. I want you to pursue your dreams and show that man he left behind his greatest accomplishment, which is you. Besides, the floor manager asked me out on a date today, and we have plans this weekend, so I won't be alone." I embraced her tightly, tears streaming down my cheeks. "Mom, I'm sorry. I thought you would turn against me. I should have known better."

Mrs. Wash rose from her seat, announcing, "Well, it seems my work here is finished; I imagine I've kept Jim waiting in the car for quite a while. Plus, it's a school night. You need to get some rest, my dear." As she made her way towards the door, I dashed over and embraced her from behind. "Ms. Wash, you are my savior. I don't think I would have gotten through the night without you." She turned around and returned the embrace. "Dear, that's what teachers are here for - to guide young students to their full potential." With that, she opened the door and turned back to add one last thing. "I have a feeling Harper will want to see you during study hall to-morrow." Before I could respond, she was already gone.

The following day, I found myself boarding the bus to school because Liam was no longer able to give me a ride. The day unfolded in its usual manner, and I didn't come across Harper at all. Yet, during study hall, an inexplicable feeling urged me to visit our usual hangout spot. I made my way to the courtyard, and underneath the familiar giant tree, I took a seat, hoping against hope to see her. However, disappointment washed over me when I didn't find her there. In reality, a part of me had yearned to reconcile with her.

Nonetheless, I settled down at our spot. Unexpectedly, Harper burst into the courtyard, and upon seeing me, she dashed towards me at full speed. Sliding to a stop in front of me, she began shouting, "I got accepted, I got accepted!" Her uncharacteristic behavior took me by surprise. "Accepted for what?" I inquired. "Mrs. Wash did it. I can't believe she did it for me!" she exclaimed. "Did what?" I prompted. With a deep breath, Harper explained, "She sent a teacher recommendation letter for me to the New Youth Scholarship board, and I got accepted to go to Colombia University!"

I gaped at her in disbelief, and together,

we jumped up, letting out shrieks of joy. I didn't care if the entire school overhead us; my best friend and I were going to college together. "I can't believe we're going to college together just like we promised." Suddenly, Harper stopped jumping, and tears started streaming down her face. "Jenny, I said terrible things to you yesterday. I'm so sorry I was a terrible friend. I should have been happy for you and not made it all about myself. I'm the worst friend in the world, and I wish I could take it all back." She couldn't bring herself to meet my eyes after saying that. Reflecting on the words of my mom and Mrs. Wash from the previous night, it became clear that this was the surprise Mrs. Wash had hinted at.

I held Harper close, feeling the weight of the confession I was about to make. Her confused expression softened as I shared the news of Liam breaking up with me the previous night and the events leading up to it. "He's going to regret it, I promise you. If he thinks he can find someone better than you, he's clearly been inhaling too many paint fumes," I said, attempting to lighten the mood. We both chuckled through our tears. "I can live without Liam, but I can't live without you, Harper. We've been friends for so long, and we're practically sisters. I can't imagine my life without you by my side. I forgive you for everything, and I hope you can forgive me for not telling you about my application to Colombia. Can we put this behind us?" Harper took my hands in hers and said, "Let's prepare for college together." We embraced each other tightly, tears of relief

and joy streaming down our faces, knowing that our friendship remained unbreakable.

Chapter 7

The summer that followed was an exhilarating whirlwind of activities and events. One memory that stands out is the day of my graduation ceremony. As I made my way across the stage to receive my diploma, I had the incredible privilege of having Mrs. Wash, the teacher who had made a profound impact on my life, hand it to me. The exchange of smiles and the warm, tight hug she gave me before presenting the certificate filled me with a deep sense of pride and achievement that I will never forget.

At that moment, as I gazed out into the audience, I locked eyes with my mother. Her exuberant shouts of my name and the sheer excitement written all over her face filled me with indescribable joy. Her pride beamed from her, and it remains one of the most joyful and memorable moments of my life.

That day not only marked the end of a significant chapter in my life but also symbolized the beginning of an exciting new one. It's a moment that has stayed with me, a cherished memory that I hold dear.

After resigning from my job, Mr. Wash extended an offer to Harper and me for a summer internship at the local police station. Our responsibilities mainly involved organizing and filing police reports, yet the exposure and knowledge gained were invaluable, allowing us to earn early college credits. While meticulously scrutinizing the reports, I unexpectedly stumbled upon a familiar name – Liam. To my astonishment, he had been apprehended for joyriding. Despite my efforts to suppress it, a subtle smile found its way to my face upon seeing his name in the police report.

Harper and I dedicated significant time shuttling between Loveland and Columbia University, eagerly navigating the intricacies of our student registration process and embarking on captivating campus tours. The university grounds were a marvel to behold, adorned with splendid architectural marvels and steeped in a storied history. As someone who had never set foot on a campus of such grandeur, the experience was profoundly fulfilling.

I vividly remember the day of the student orientation, with the air filled with a mixture of excitement and nervous energy. It was during this orientation that Harper and I discovered we had been assigned to the same dorm room, much to our delight. Walking into our dorm for the first time, we were greeted by a cozy, albeit small, space. Each of us had a comfortable bed, a spacious desk, and a little nook for our personal belongings.

As I stood in the room, I couldn't help but envision little ways to make it feel more like home. I planned on placing a picture of myself, Mrs. Wash and my mom on the desk to remind me of home. I longed for a little deck where I could place some

Daylilies in a pot, allowing their sweet scent to evoke memories of home.

Despite my musings, I was eager to kick off the semester and embark on this new chapter of my life. Yet, I knew that it was time to head back to Loveland for the rest of the summer to cherish the moments with my mom and make the most of our time together.

As the summer gradually drew to a close, a mix of excitement and apprehension bubbled within me. The day had finally arrived for my departure to the airport, marking the beginning of my journey to college and the start of classes next week. All of my bags were meticulously packed, and even though my mom was trying hard to hold back her emotions, I could see the tears welling up in her eyes. This stirred a profound sense of sadness within me as well. For the past 18 years, she had been a constant presence in my life, and now I was about to wake up in a dorm room far from home. The thought of not seeing her every day and not waking up to her making our lunches was tough to process.

As I got ready to leave for college, I had a heartfelt conversation with my mom. I reassured her that everything would be alright and made a promise to return during fall break. My mom wiped away her tears and shared that she had been steeling herself for this day throughout the entire summer, yet it still proved difficult. She acknowledged that every parent must eventually come to terms with the reality that their child will one day leave the nest, but that realization didn't make it any easier.

As we sat together reflecting on the years gone by, I noticed my mom's voice quiver, struggling to hold back tears. She spoke about how, not too long ago, my sister Harper and I were young kids racing through the halls of our home, and now we were two young adults about to embark on our college journeys. She acknowledged the hard work she had put into raising me single-handedly, especially after my dad left us.

Feeling the weight of my emotions, I confessed to my mom how deeply hurt I was that my dad hadn't shown up to my graduation, and I felt the tears welling up. At that moment, my mom reached out and placed her hands on my shoulders, comforting me. She assured me that I was the greatest gift my dad had ever given to the world and that his biggest mistake was leaving me behind. She reminded me that this was something he would have to live with.

This summer, I noticed a positive change in my mom's demeanor, and I had a hunch that her new boyfriend, Robert, was the reason behind it. Robert, the floor manager at the potato processing plant, had recently asked my mom out. Her spirits seemed to have lifted, and I was genuinely happy to see her in such high spirits. I expressed my joy at seeing her so content and assured her of my love.

My mom's face lit up with a radiant smile as she mentioned that Robert had intended to give me something as well, but he was called in to work. She reached into her bag and pulled out a striking golden potato statue adorned with a plaque that proudly proclaimed, "Loveland, home of the greatest potatoes." We both shared a hearty laugh, and I carefully stowed the unique souvenir in my suitcase. Just before leaving, I embraced my mom and promised to call her as soon as I settled into college.

As I held her close, I could feel her trembling against me, her warmth and familiar scent surrounding me. I struggled to contain my own emotions, knowing that showing weakness would only make it more difficult for both of us. Despite the inner turmoil, I forced myself to remain composed, swallowing the lump in my throat and blinking back tears. Mrs. Wash's words echoed in my mind, reminding me to be strong and self-reliant.

Standing at the doorway, my mother and I were suddenly interrupted by the blaring sound of a car horn, signaling the arrival of my taxi van. Hastily collecting my bags, I made my way towards the waiting vehicle, where Harper was already settled, her belongings neatly stowed in the back. Our decision to travel together was a combination of practicality and mutual support, ensuring our safety as we embarked on our journey to the airport.

As I prepared to depart, my mother stood by my side, assisting me in loading my luggage into the back of the taxi. With the driver's help, we secured everything in place. As I gathered my things and readied myself to leave, my mother embraced me tightly, her eyes glistening with tears. It was an emotional moment as I ventured away from home for the very first time. Despite the sadness, I knew that this departure was necessary for my growth.

Driving through Loveland, a rush of nostalgia swept over me. The city held a special significance in my heart, and in that moment, I realized that it was the amalgamation of both joyous and challenging experiences that had sculpted me into the person I am today.

As Loveland gradually vanished from view, I turned for one final glimpse of the familiar mountains that greeted me each morning. I cherished the fading scent of Daylilies, knowing it would soon be out of reach. Bidding farewell to Loveland, Ohio, I couldn't help but feel the poignant mix of emotions; a longing to return someday lingered within me.

About the author

Atticus Blackwood is a talented author hailing from Athens, GA, whose literary works seamlessly blend the genres of realistic fiction, mystery, and supernatural elements, creating a captivating and unique reading experience. His stories transport both young adult and adult readers to immersive worlds that skillfully merge the ordinary with the extraordinary, weaving together suspense and intrigue. Atticus is known for his writing style, which effortlessly combines a casual and approachable tone with expert storytelling prowess, allowing readers to deeply connect with his well-crafted characters and enthralling narratives. Fueled by a deep-seated passion for creating compelling adventures, Atticus has the remarkable ability to transform everyday moments into extraordinary tales that continue to resonate with readers long after they've finished reading.